KATE PRENDERGAST

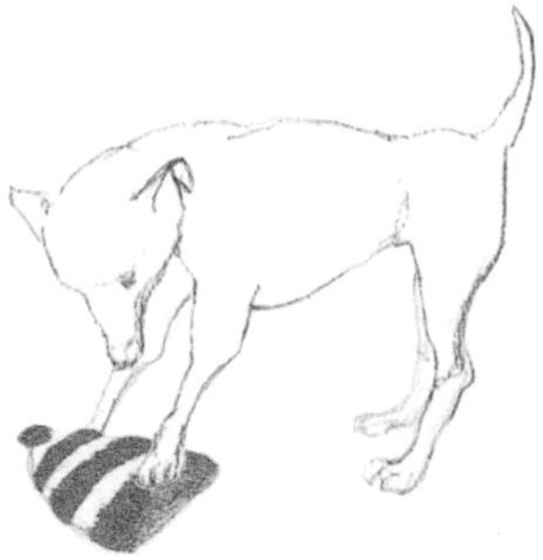

DOG ON A TRAIN

Old Barn Books

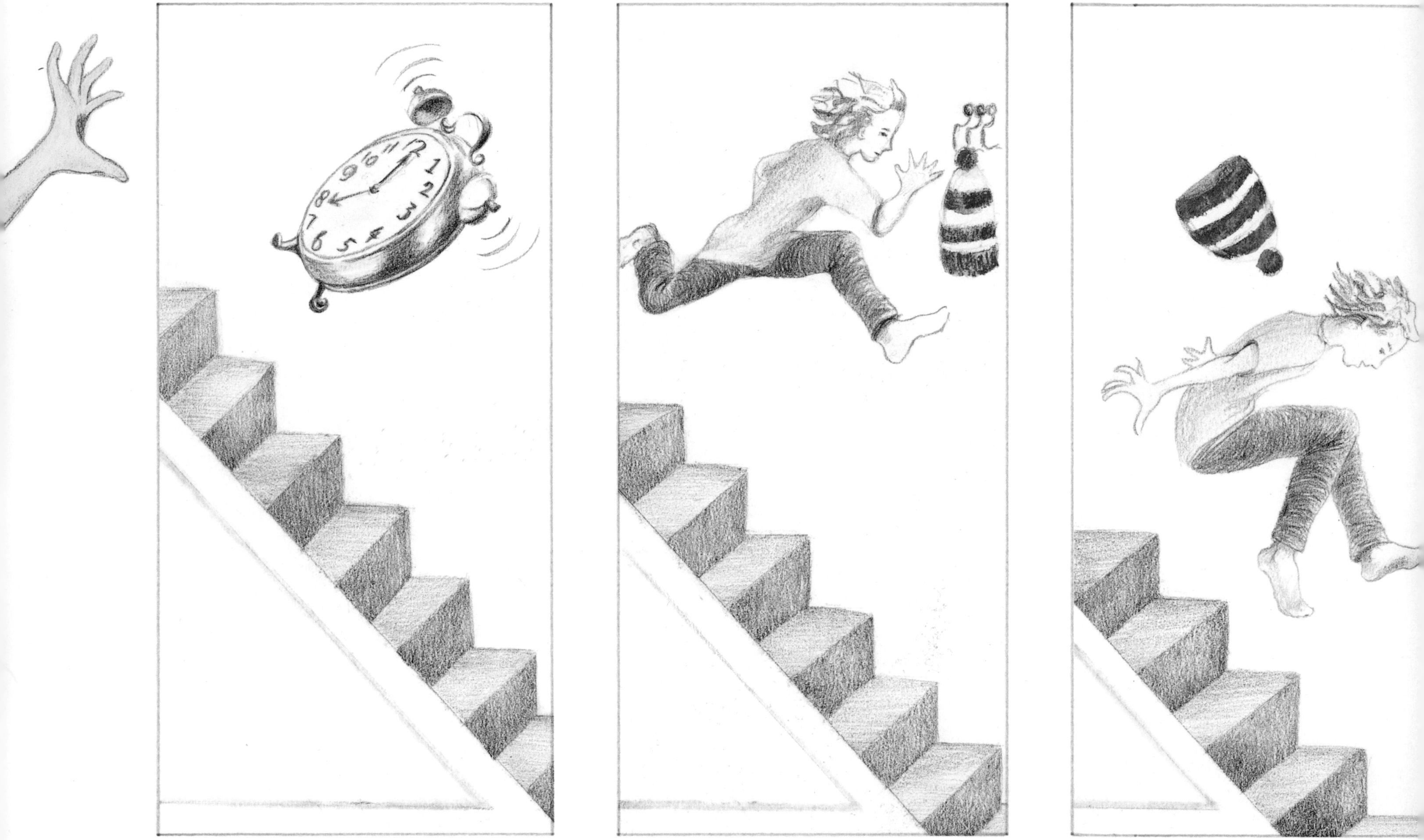

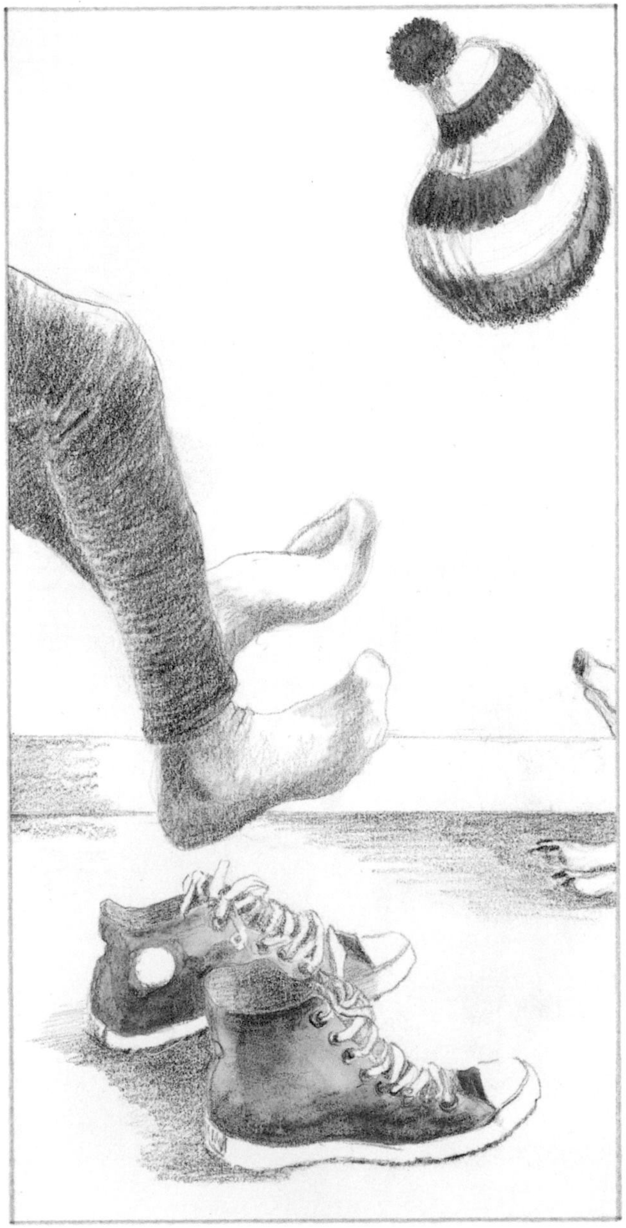
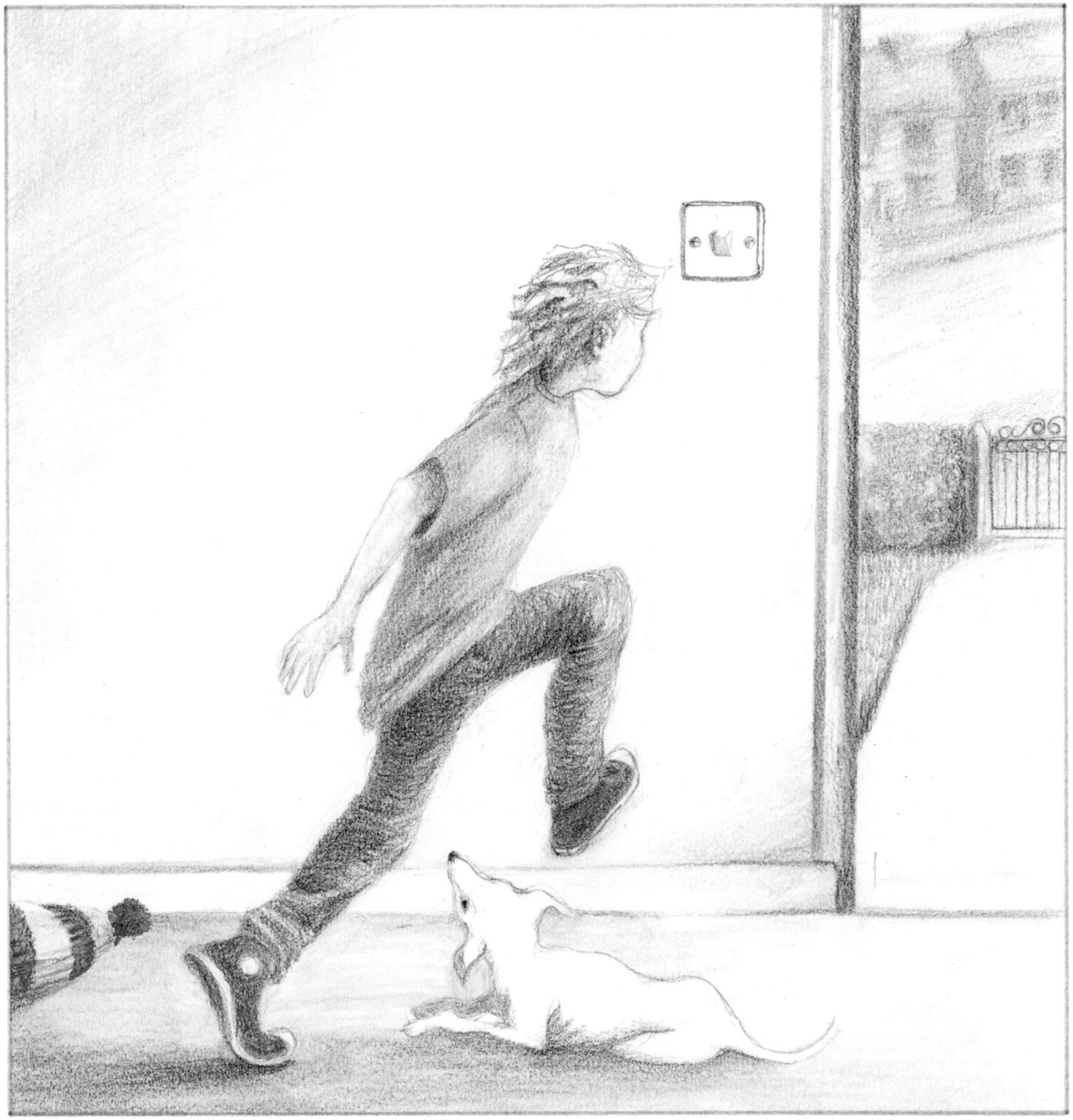

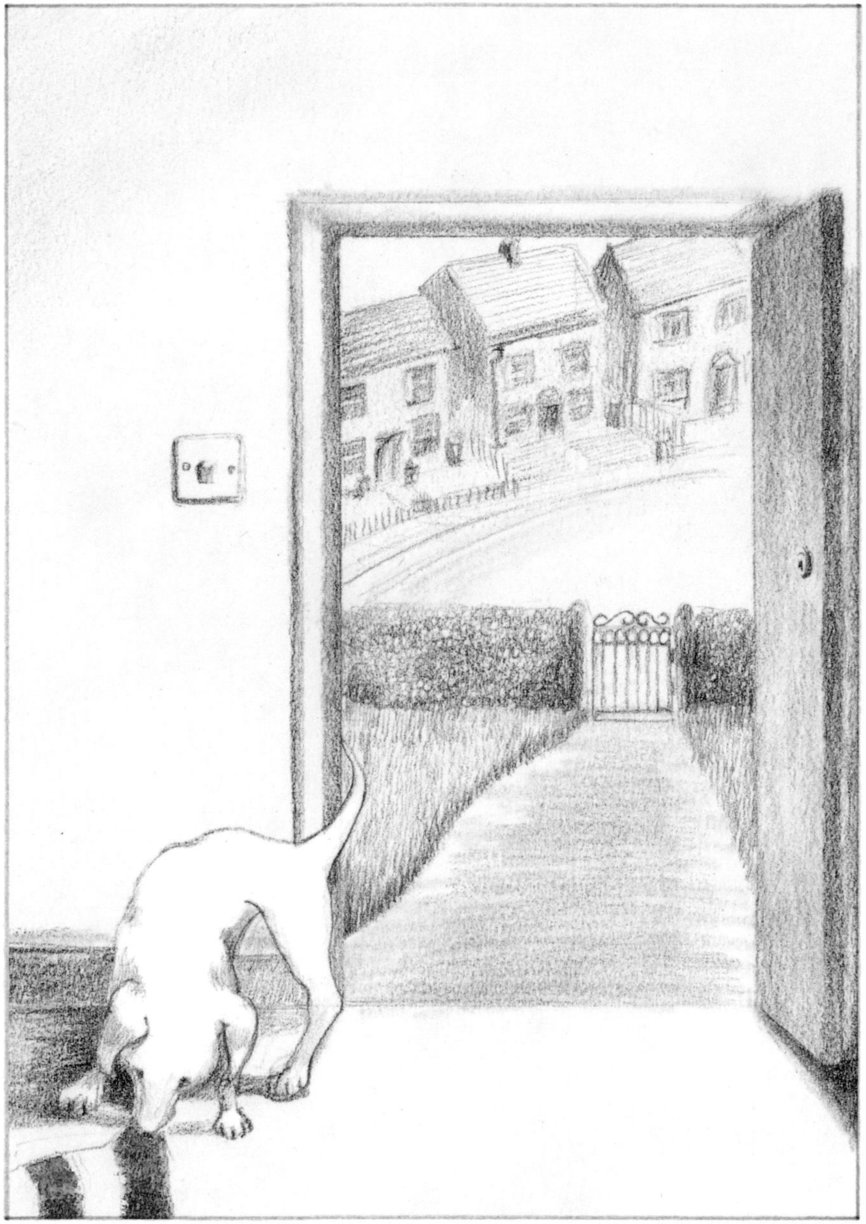
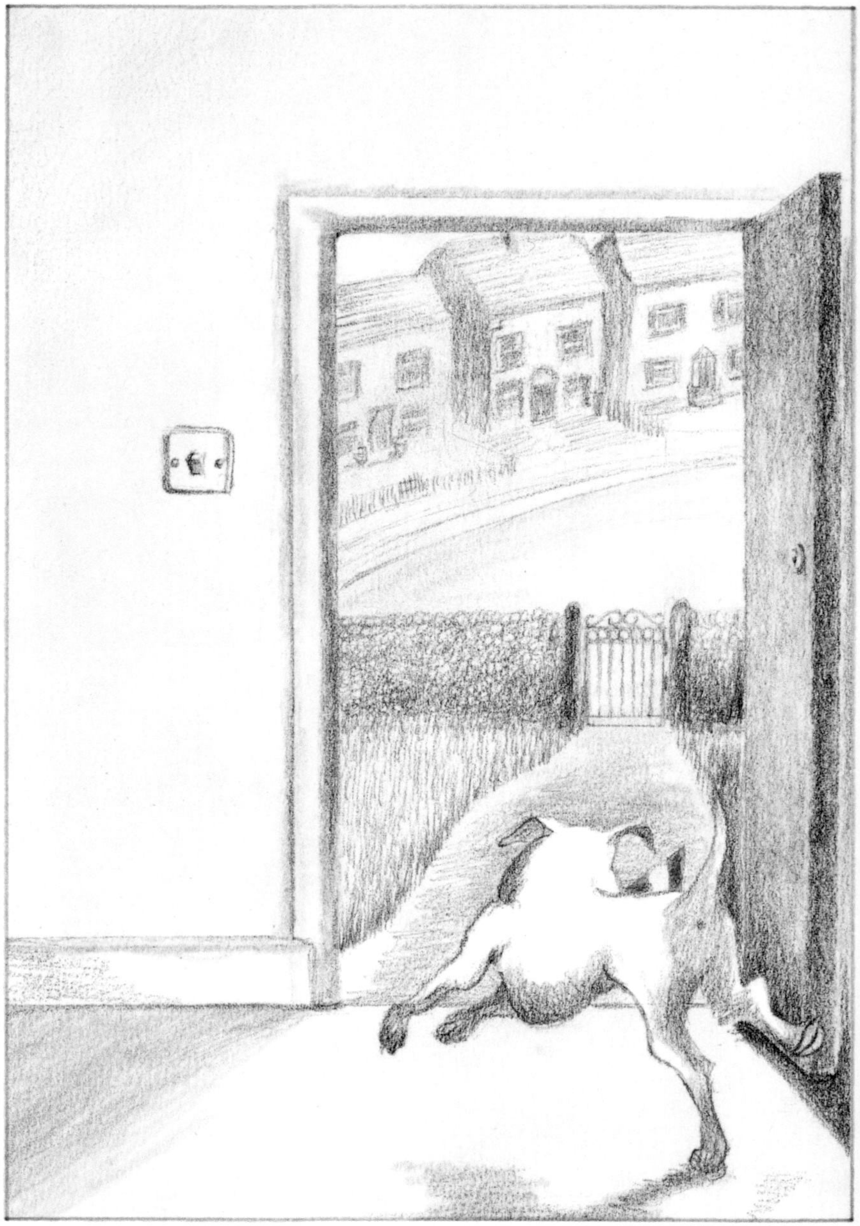

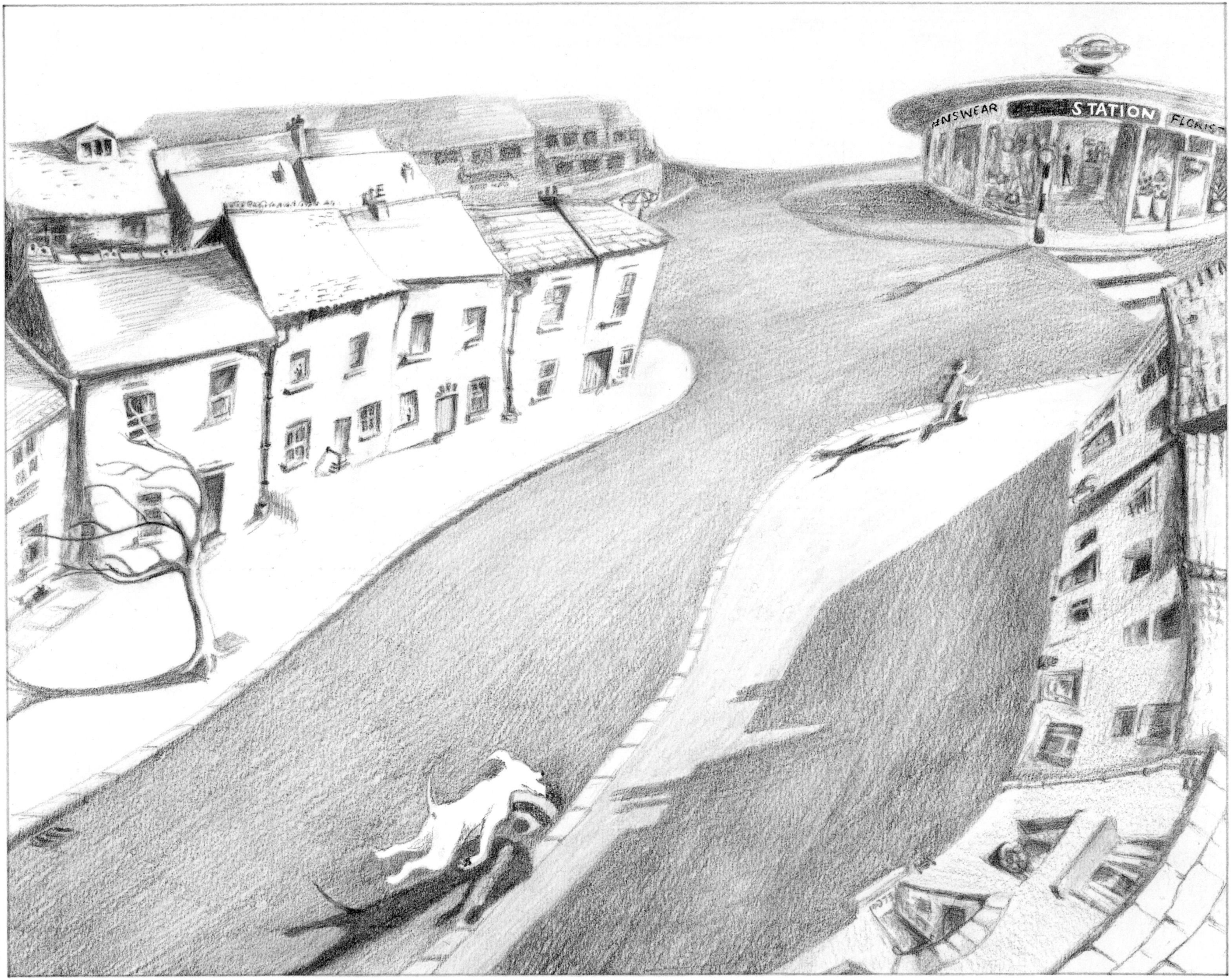
NSWEAR
STATION
FLORIST

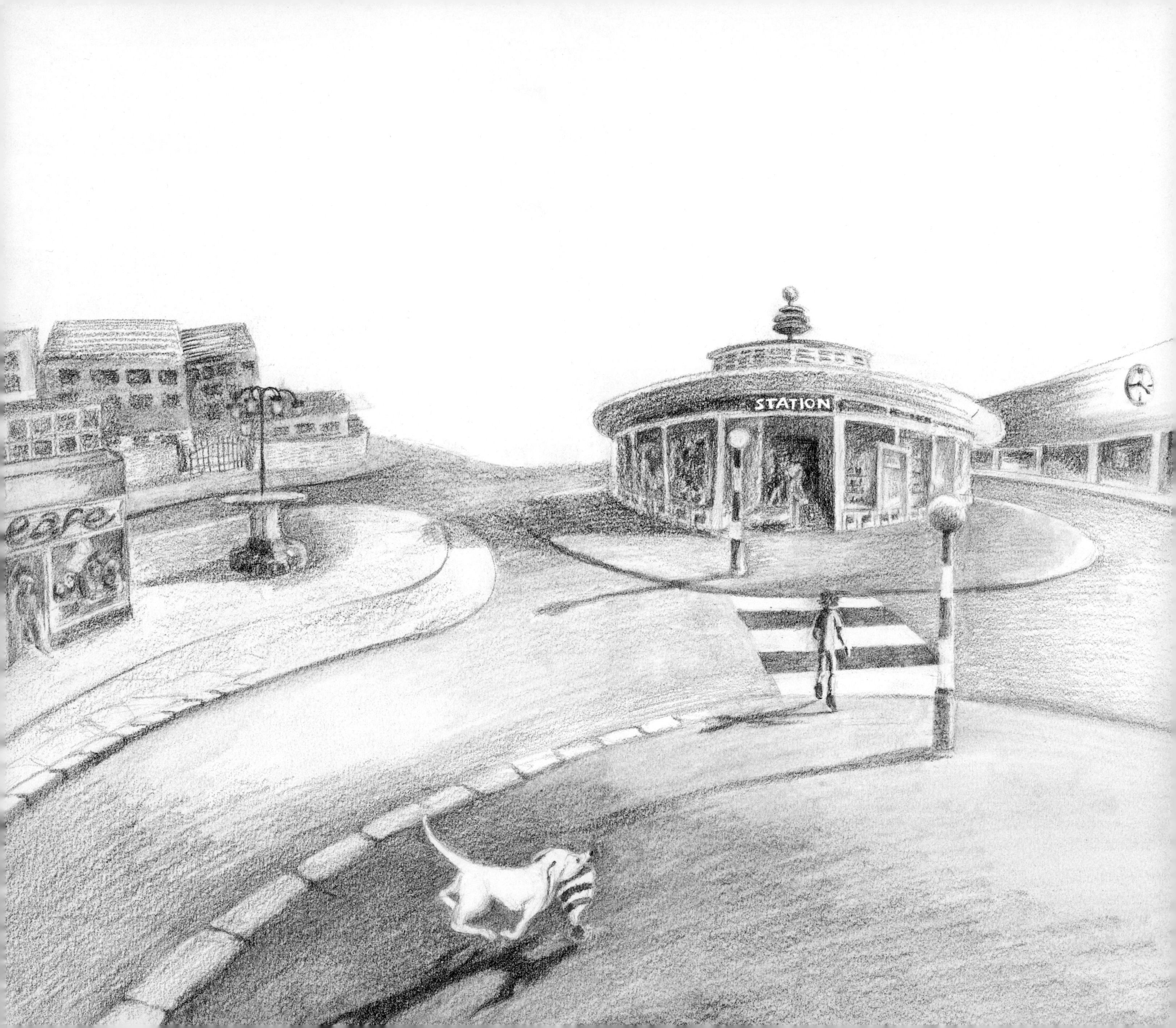
STATION

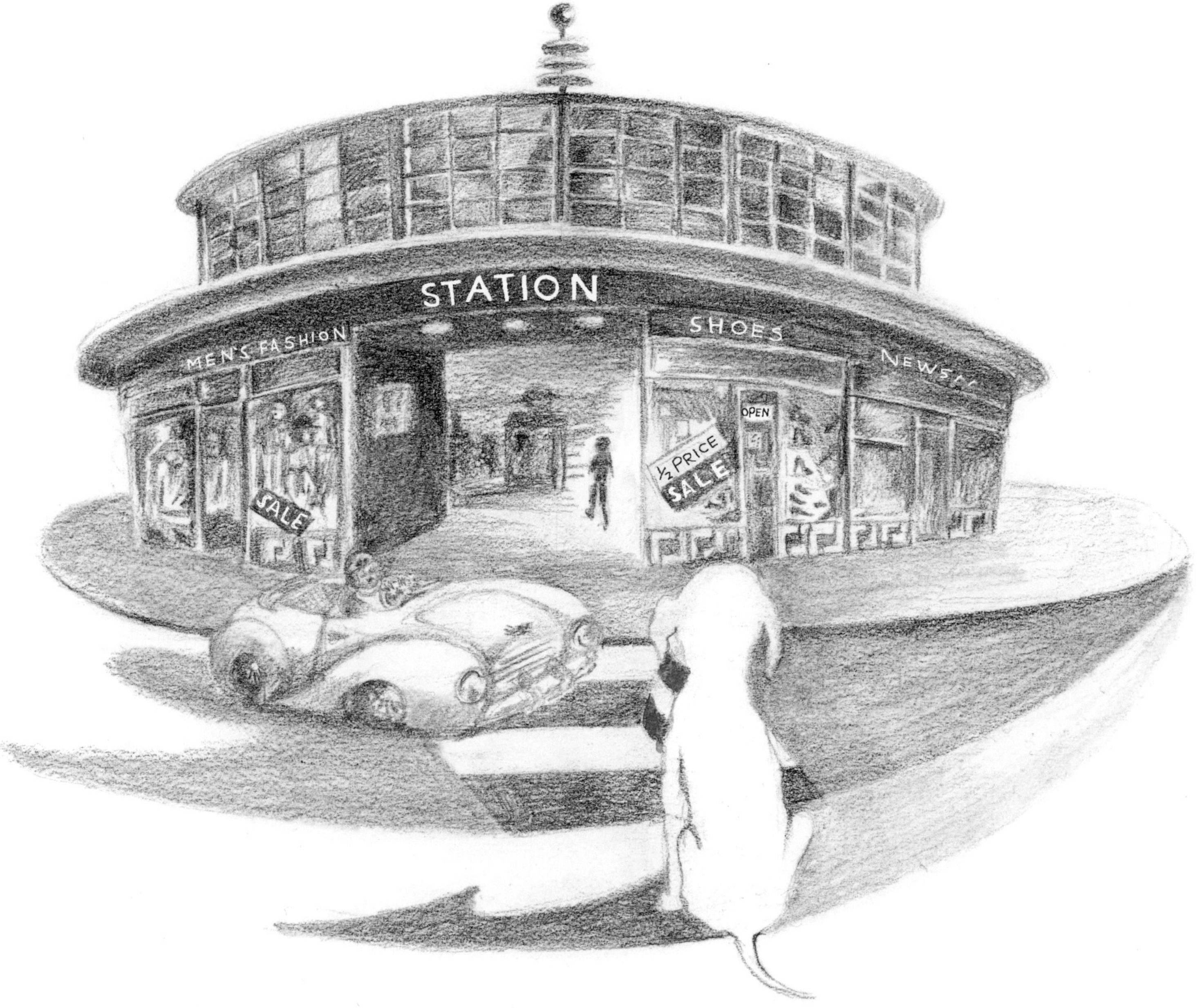
STATION
MEN'S FASHION
SHOES
OPEN
½ PRICE SALE
SALE

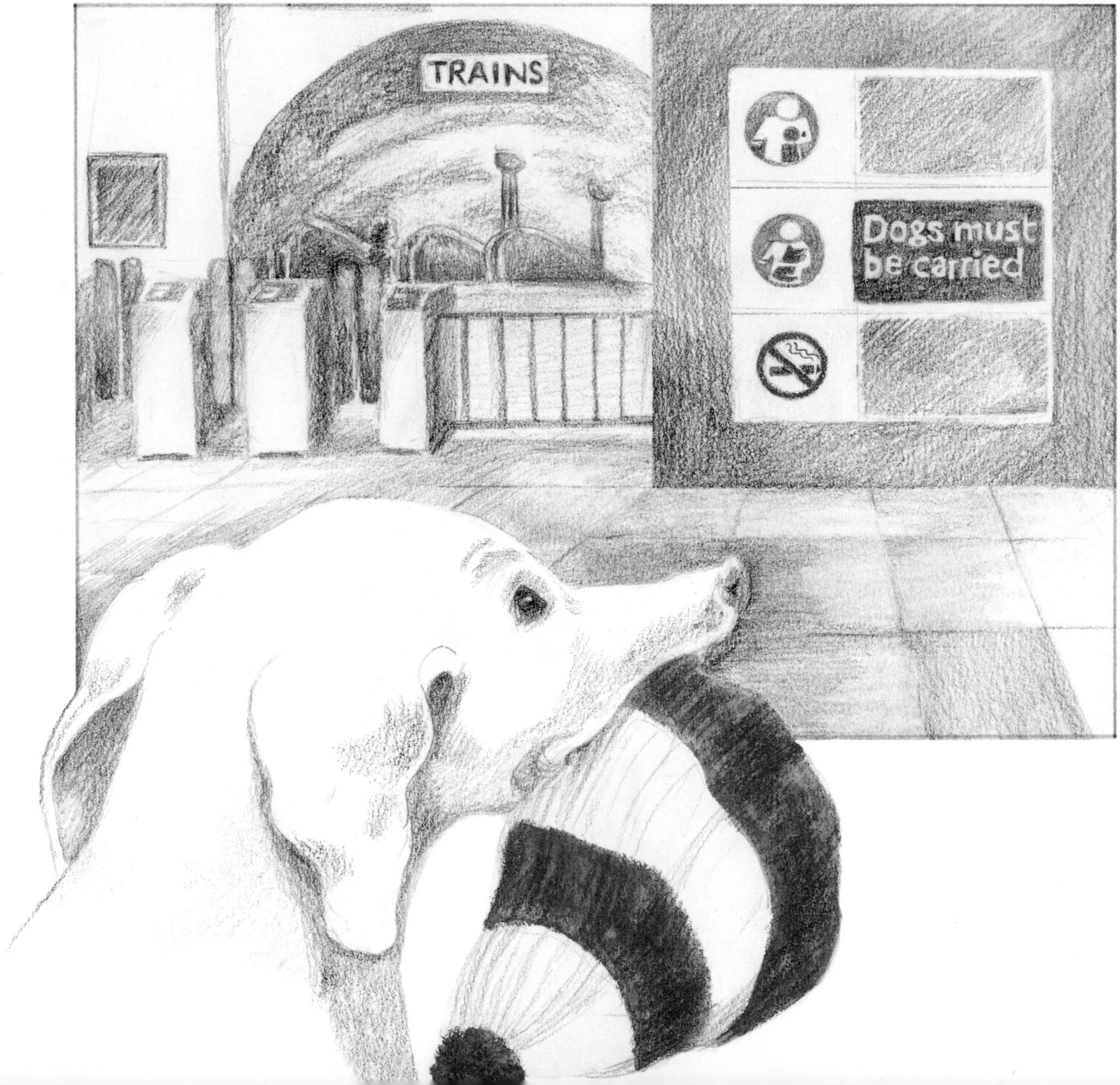

TRAINS
Dogs must be carried

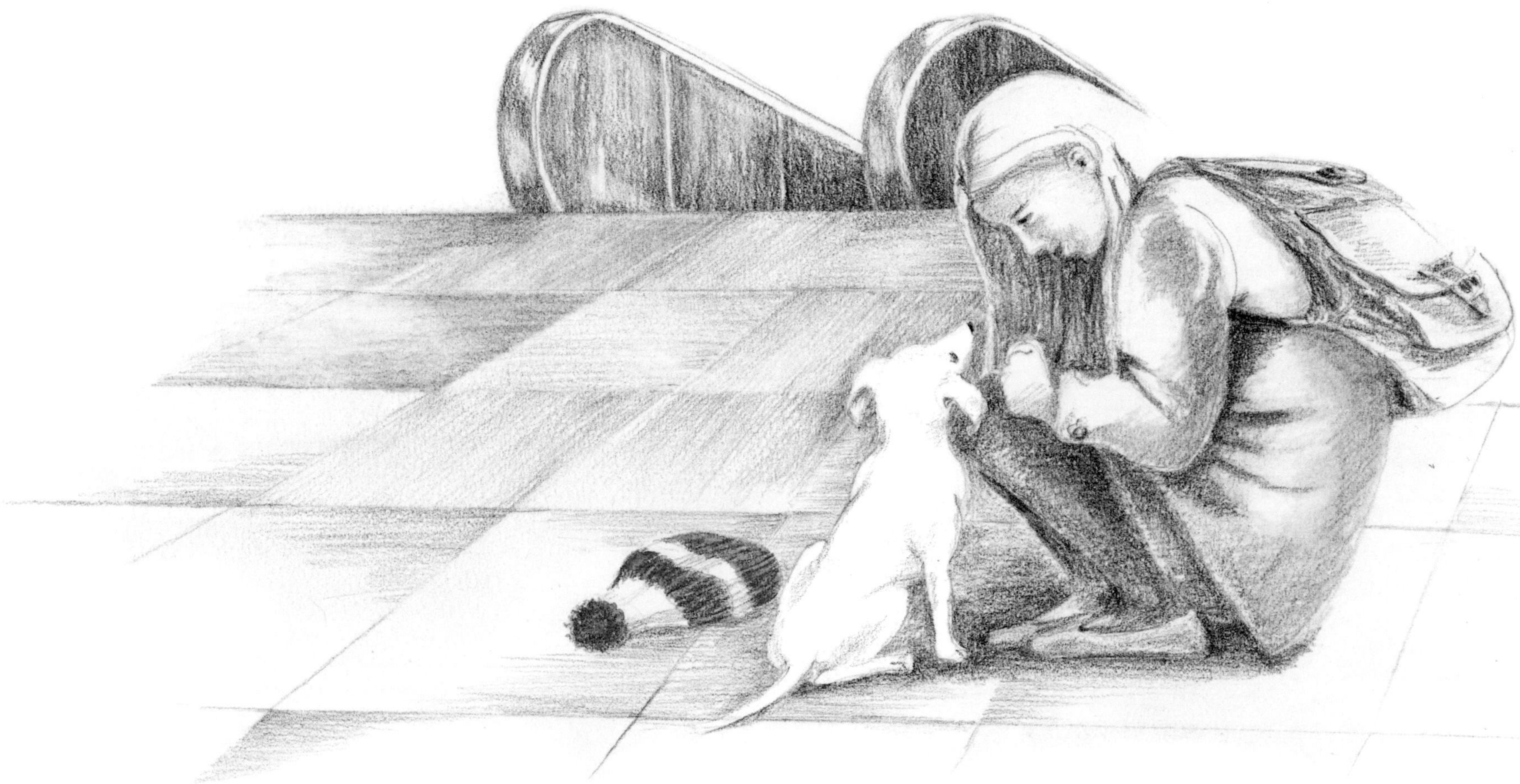

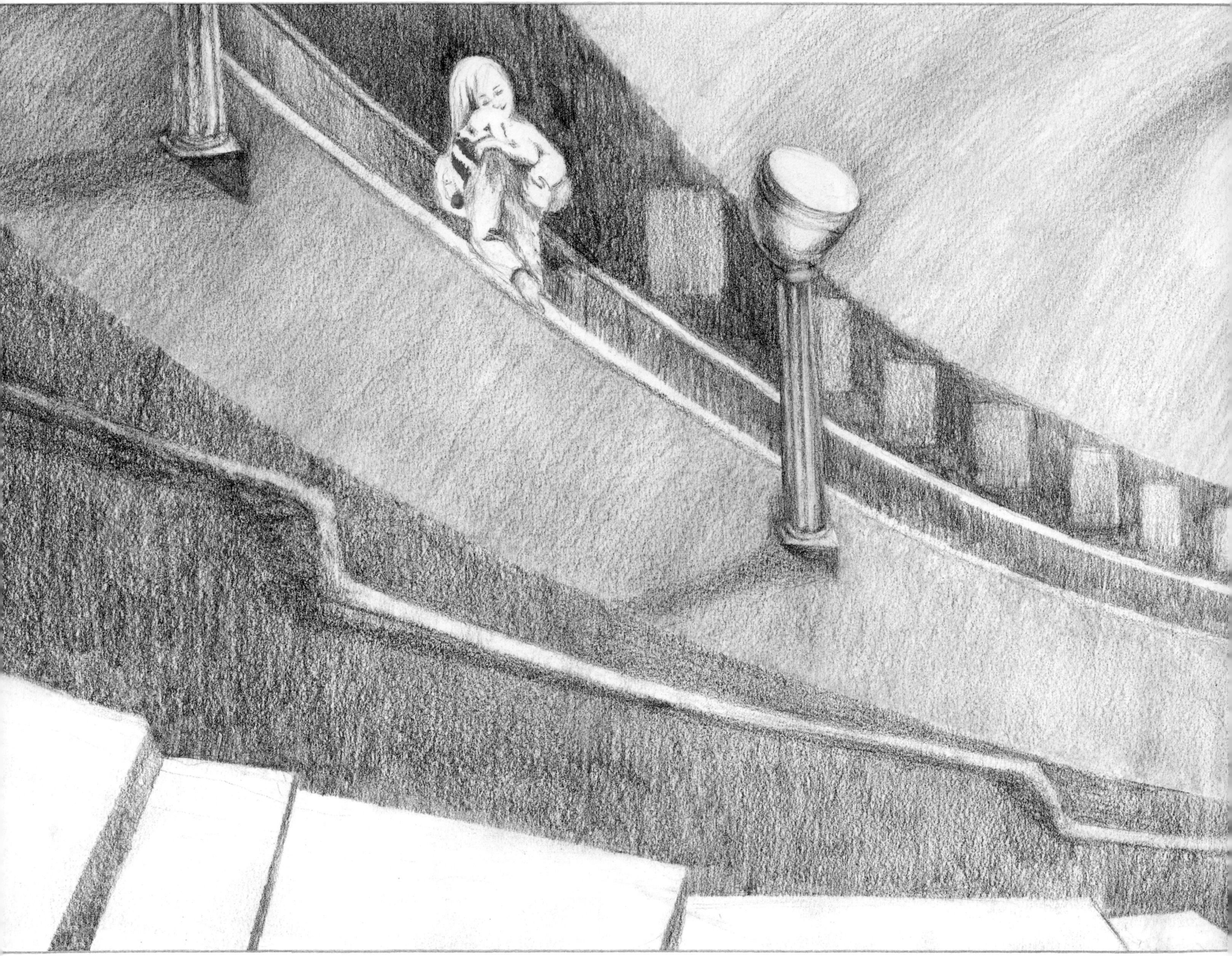

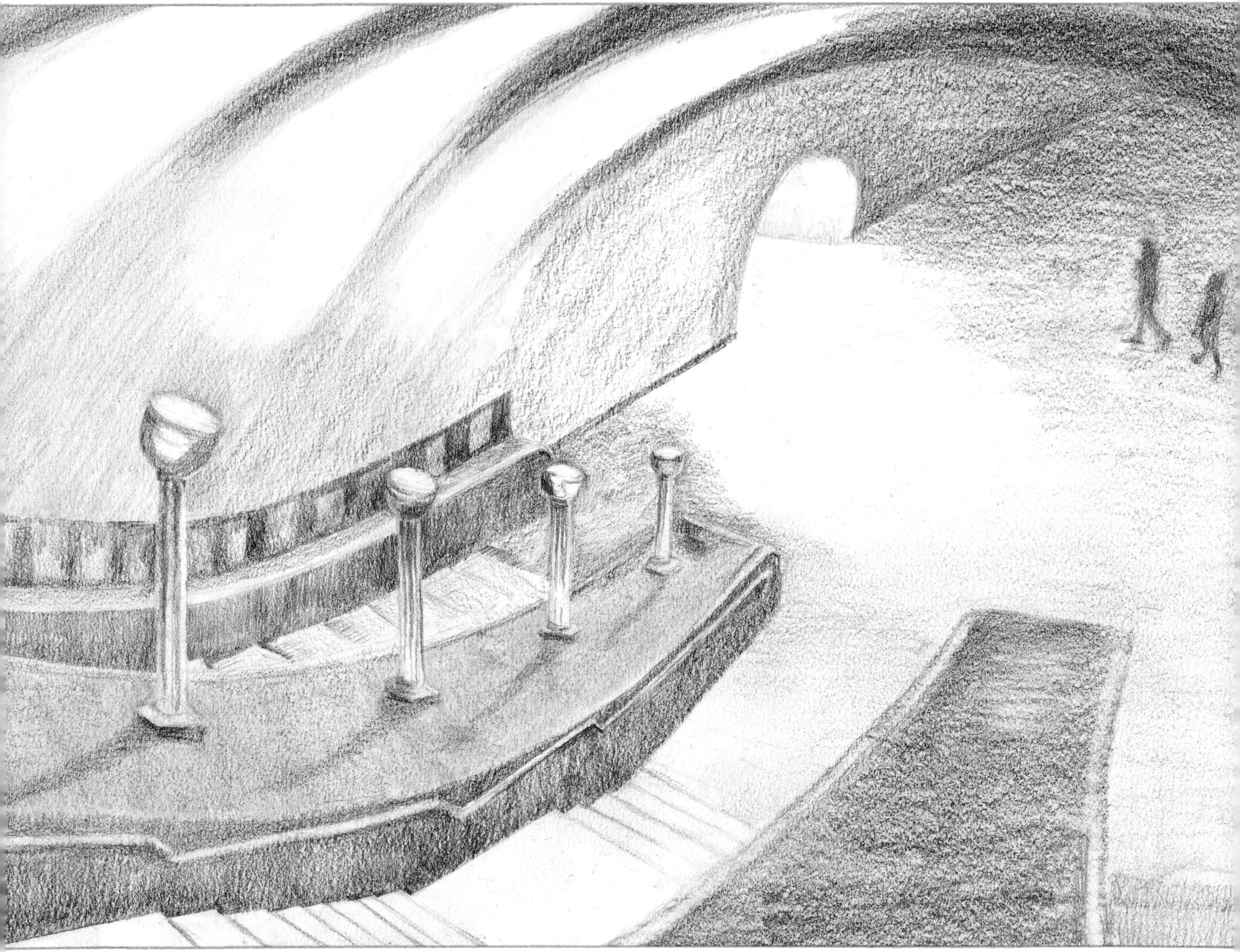

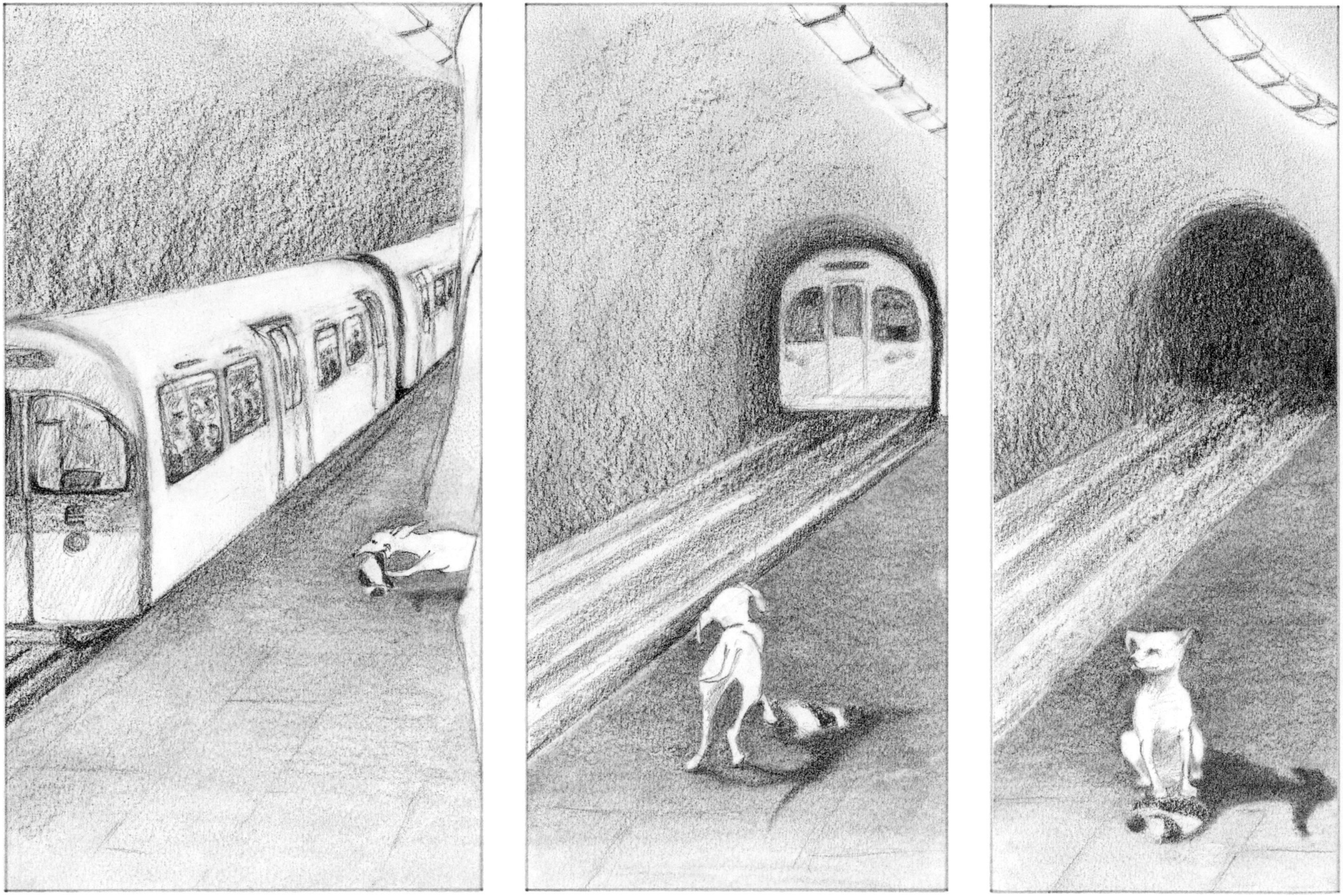

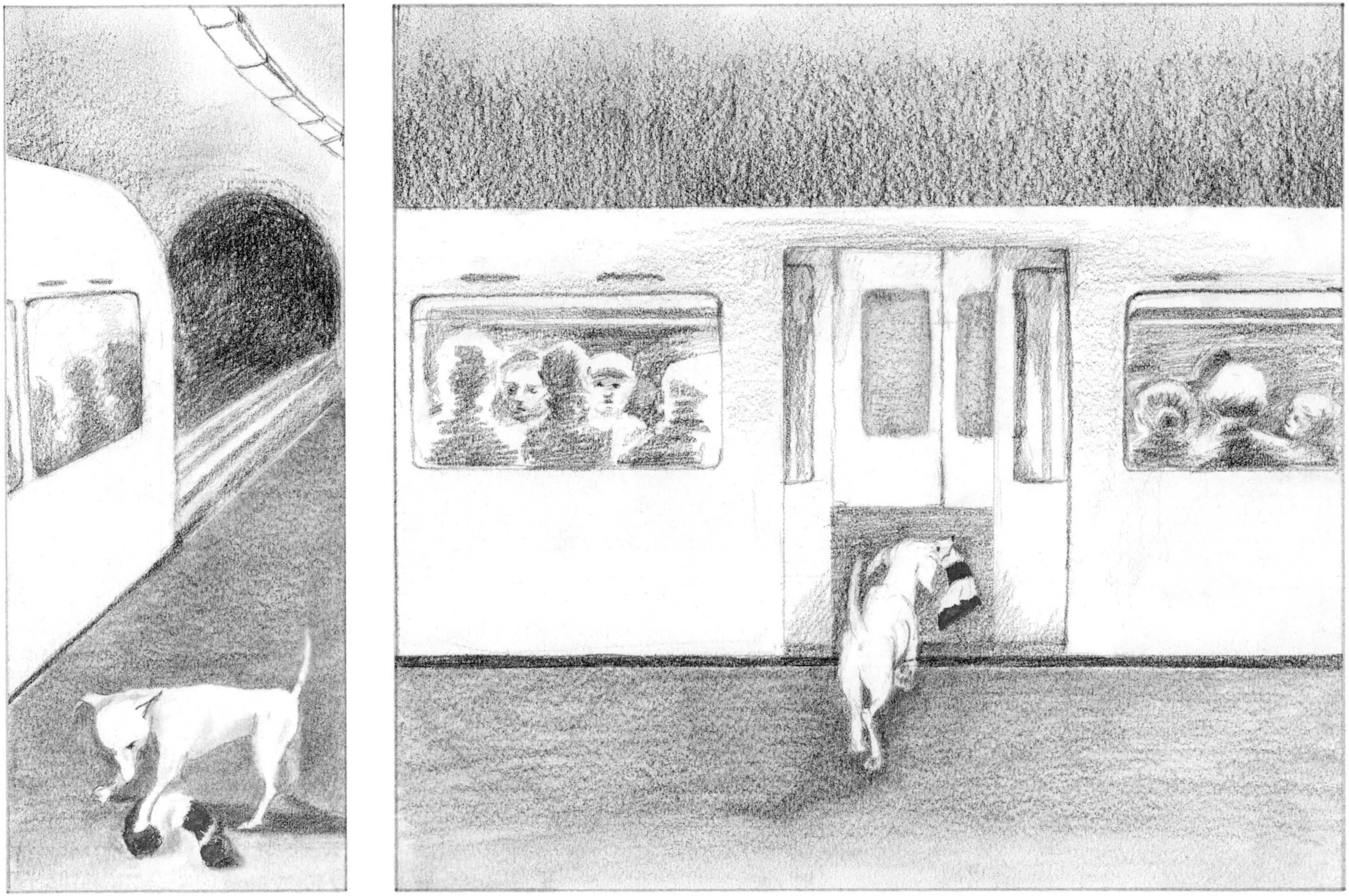

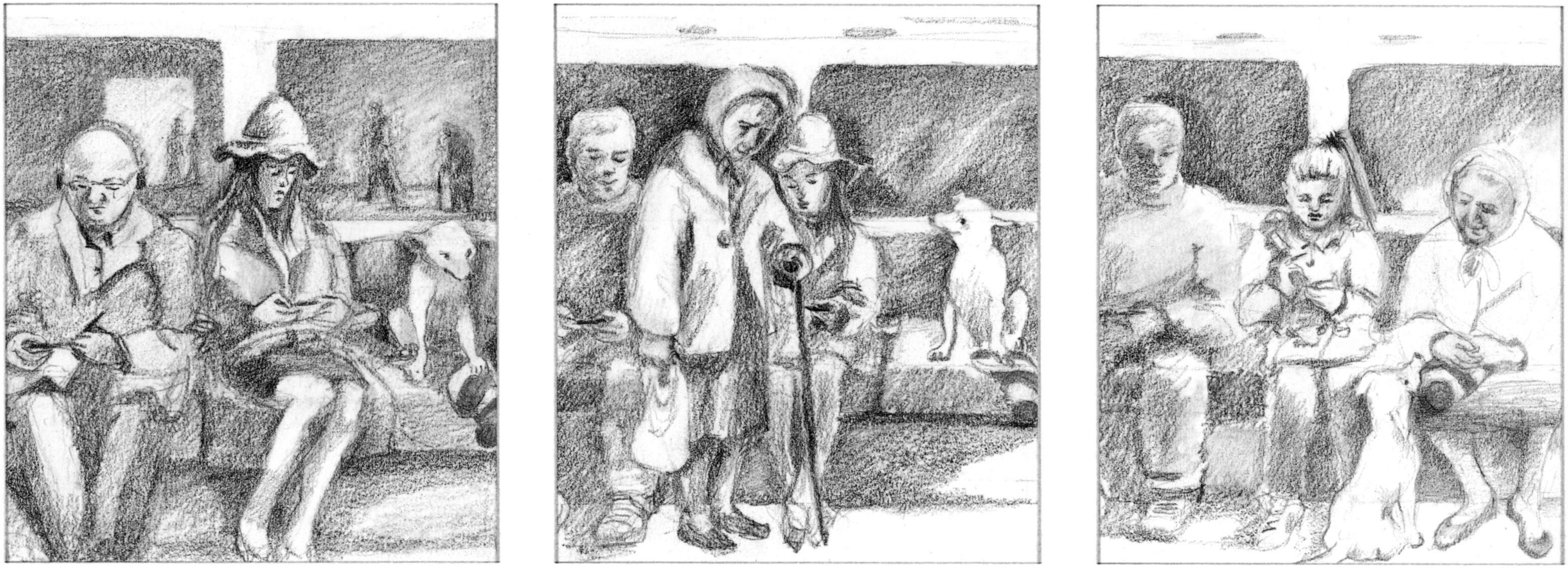

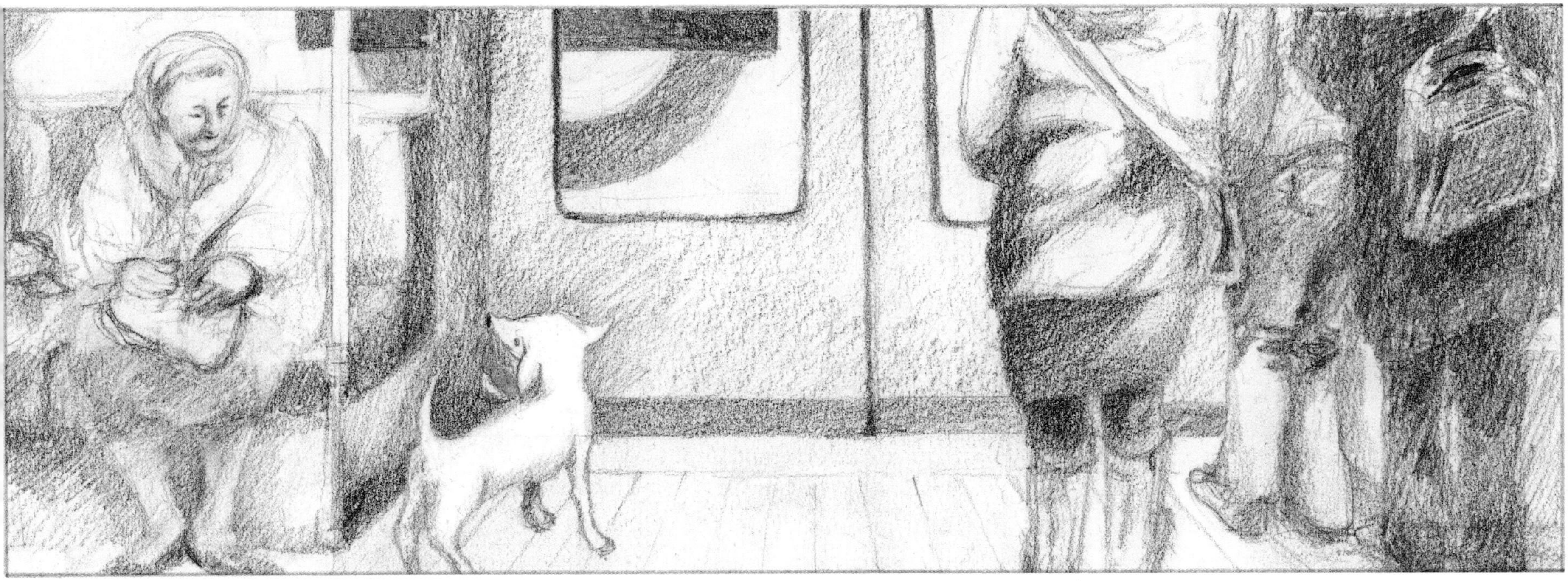

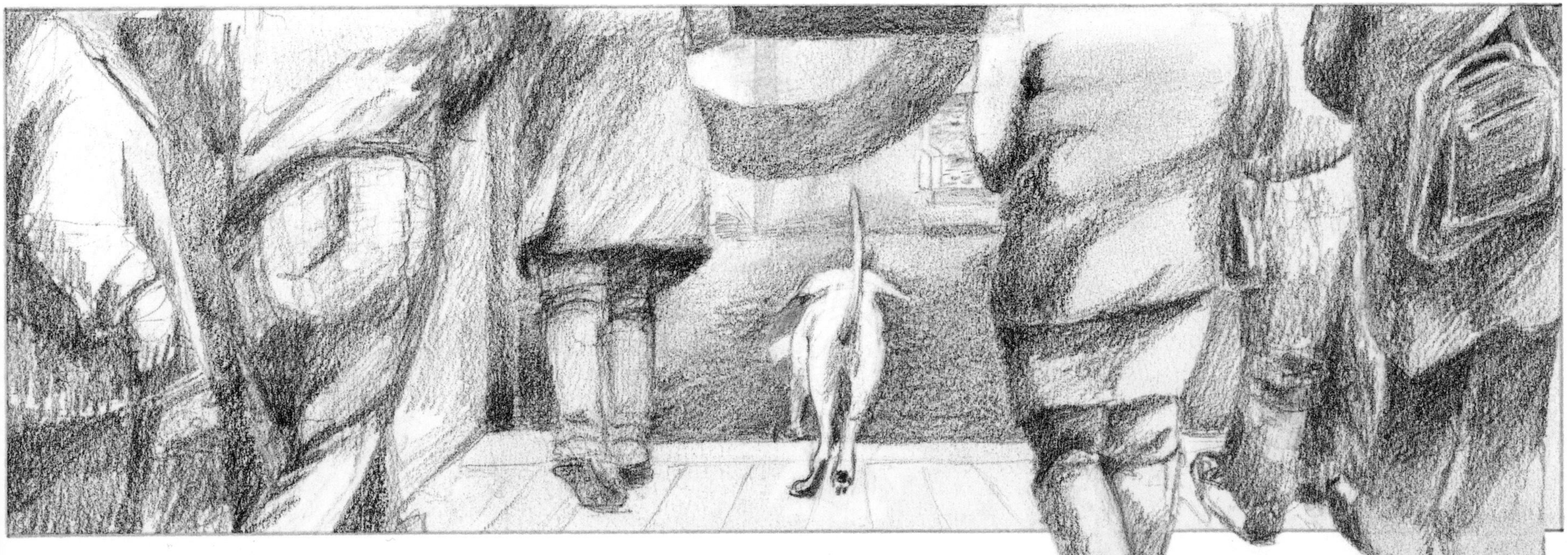

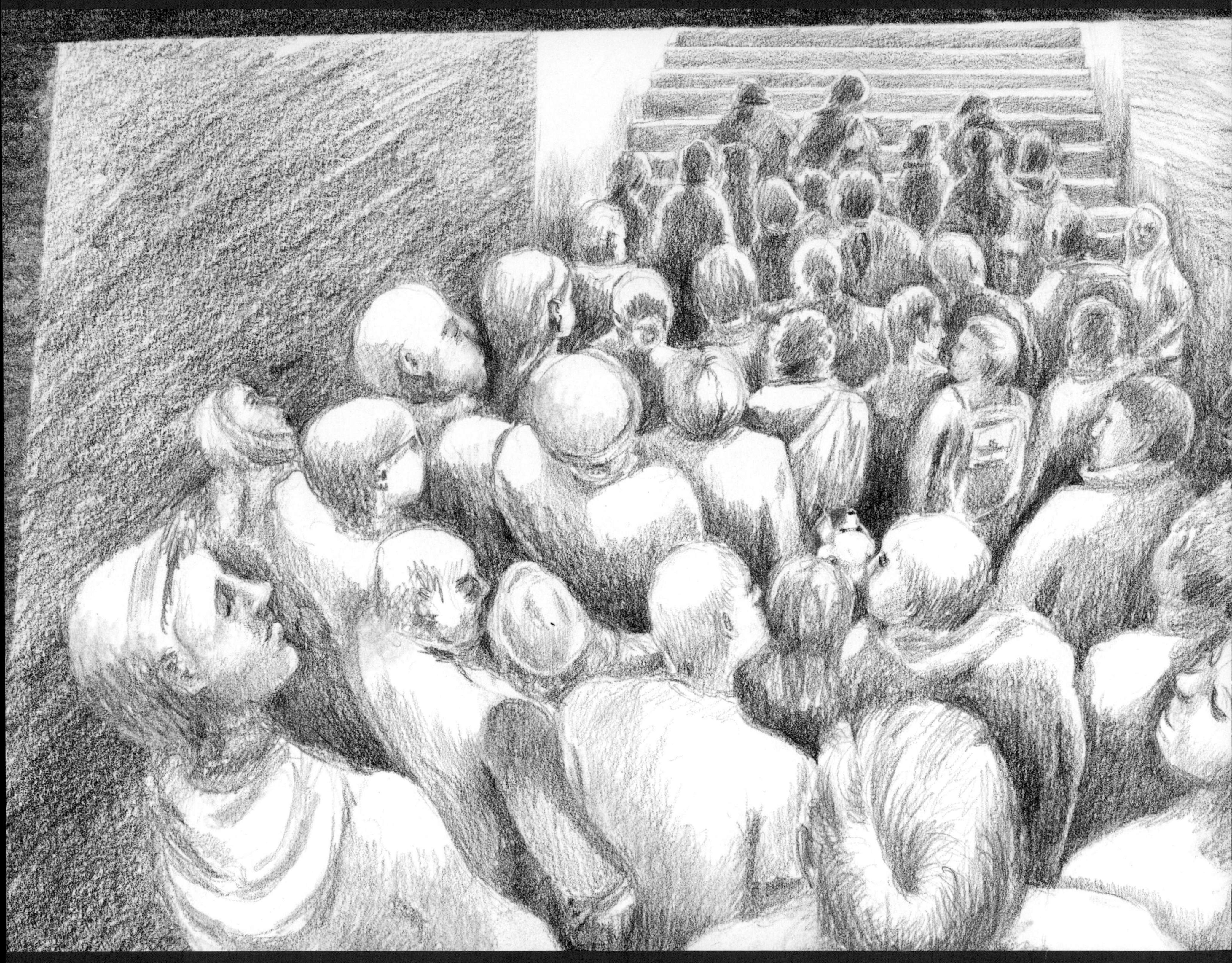

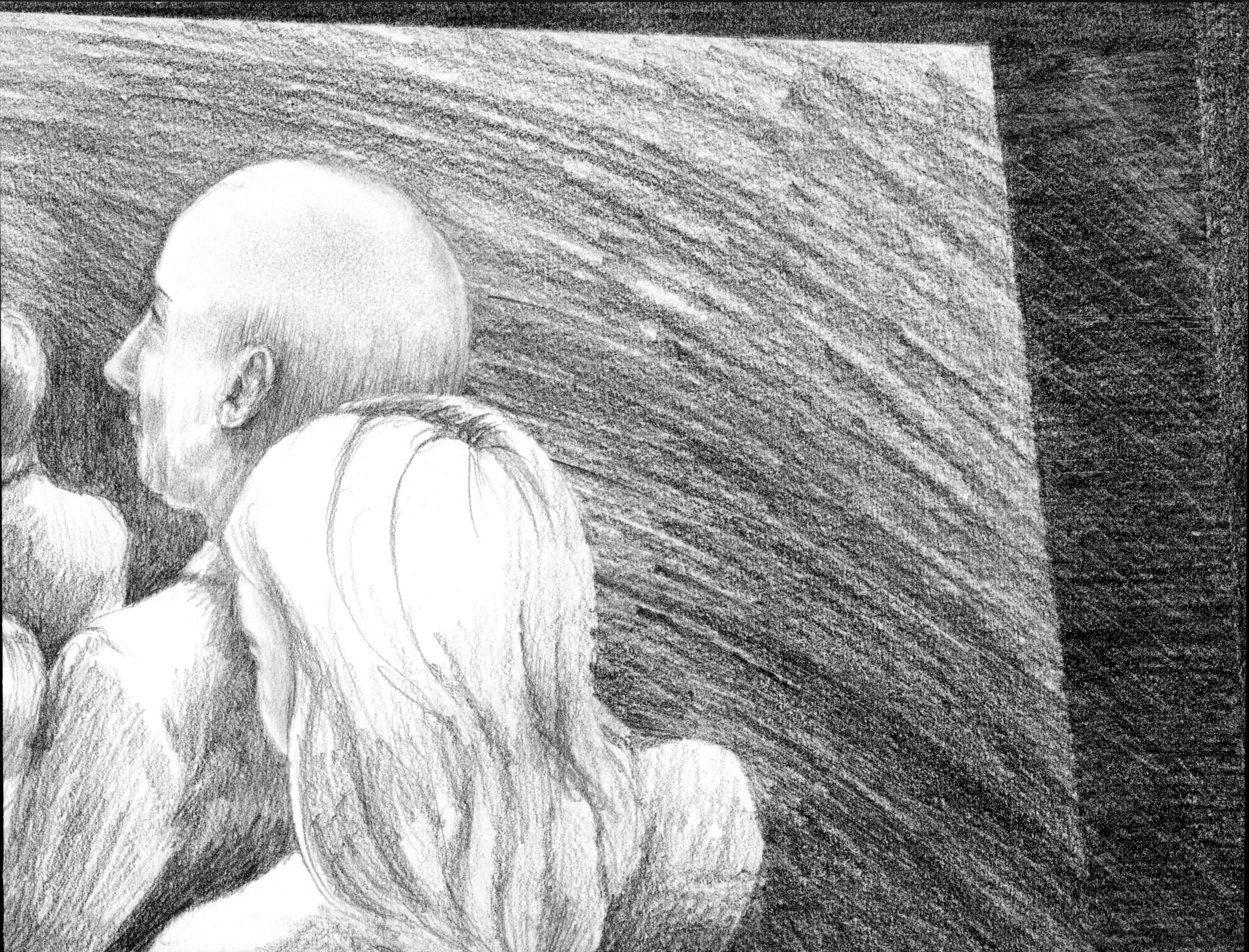

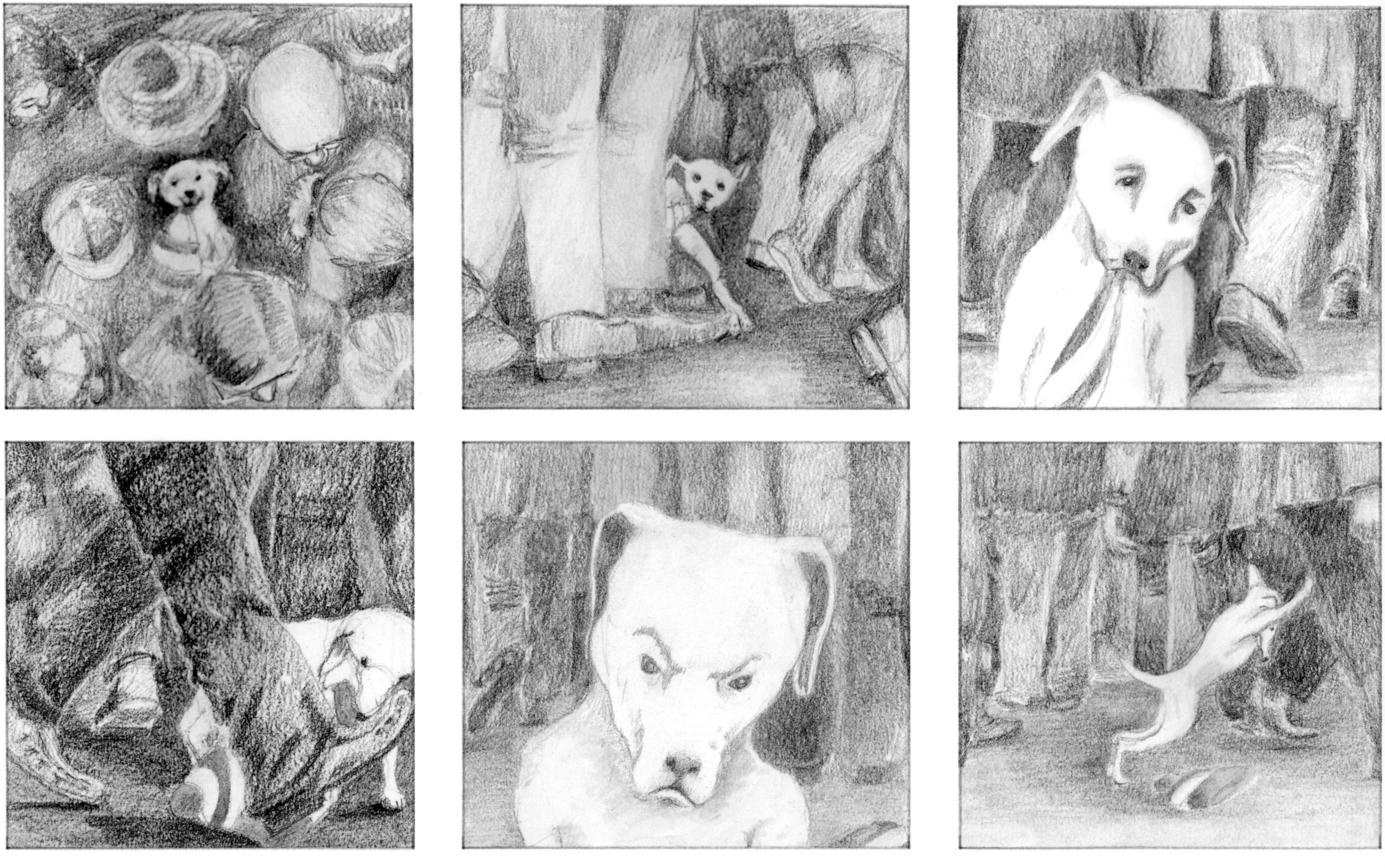

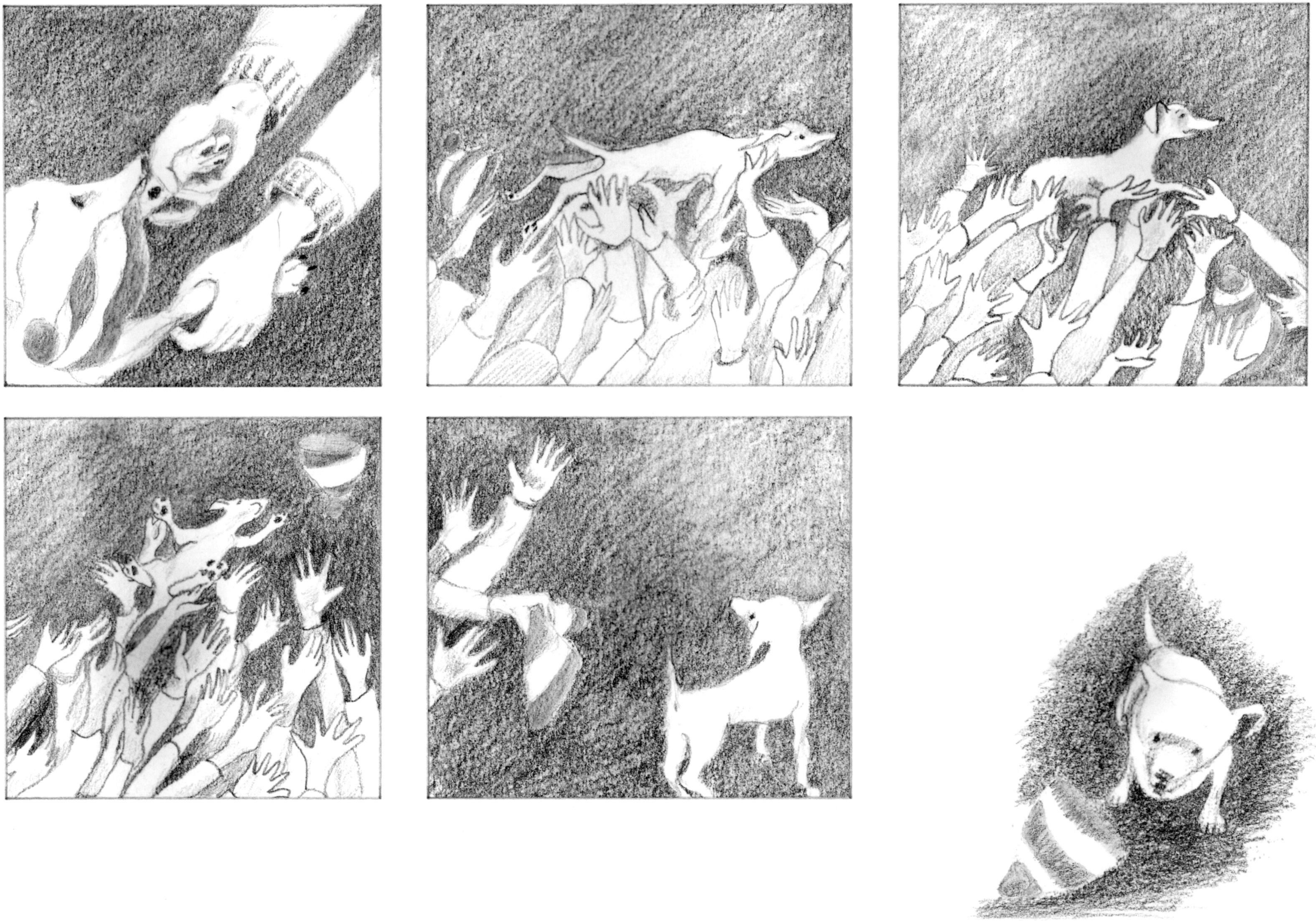

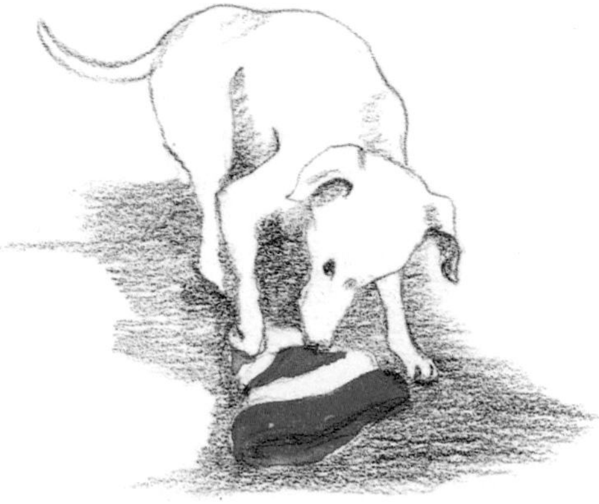
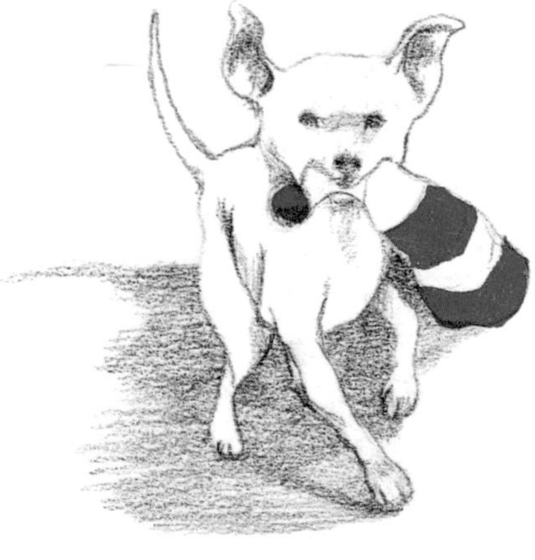
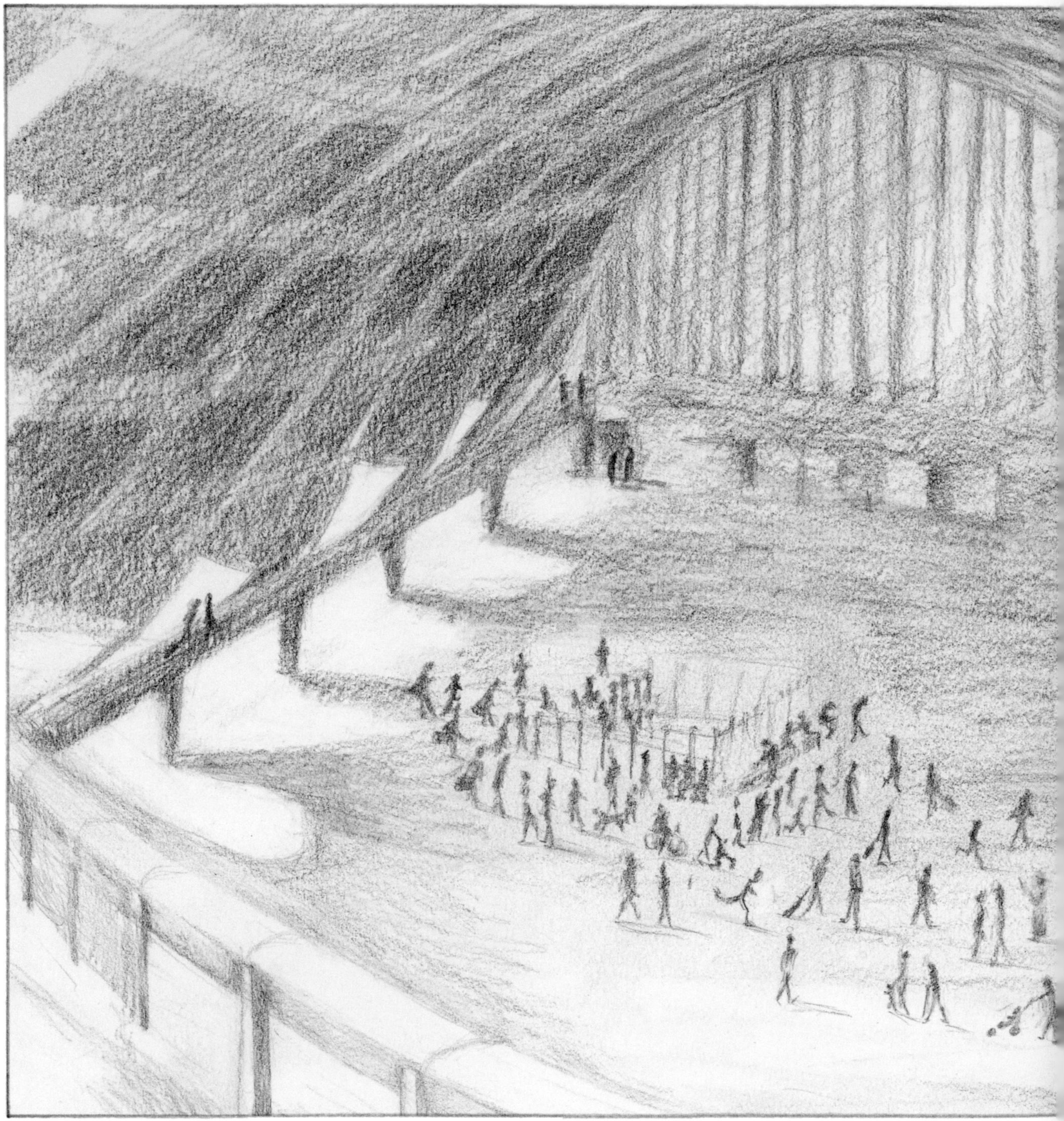

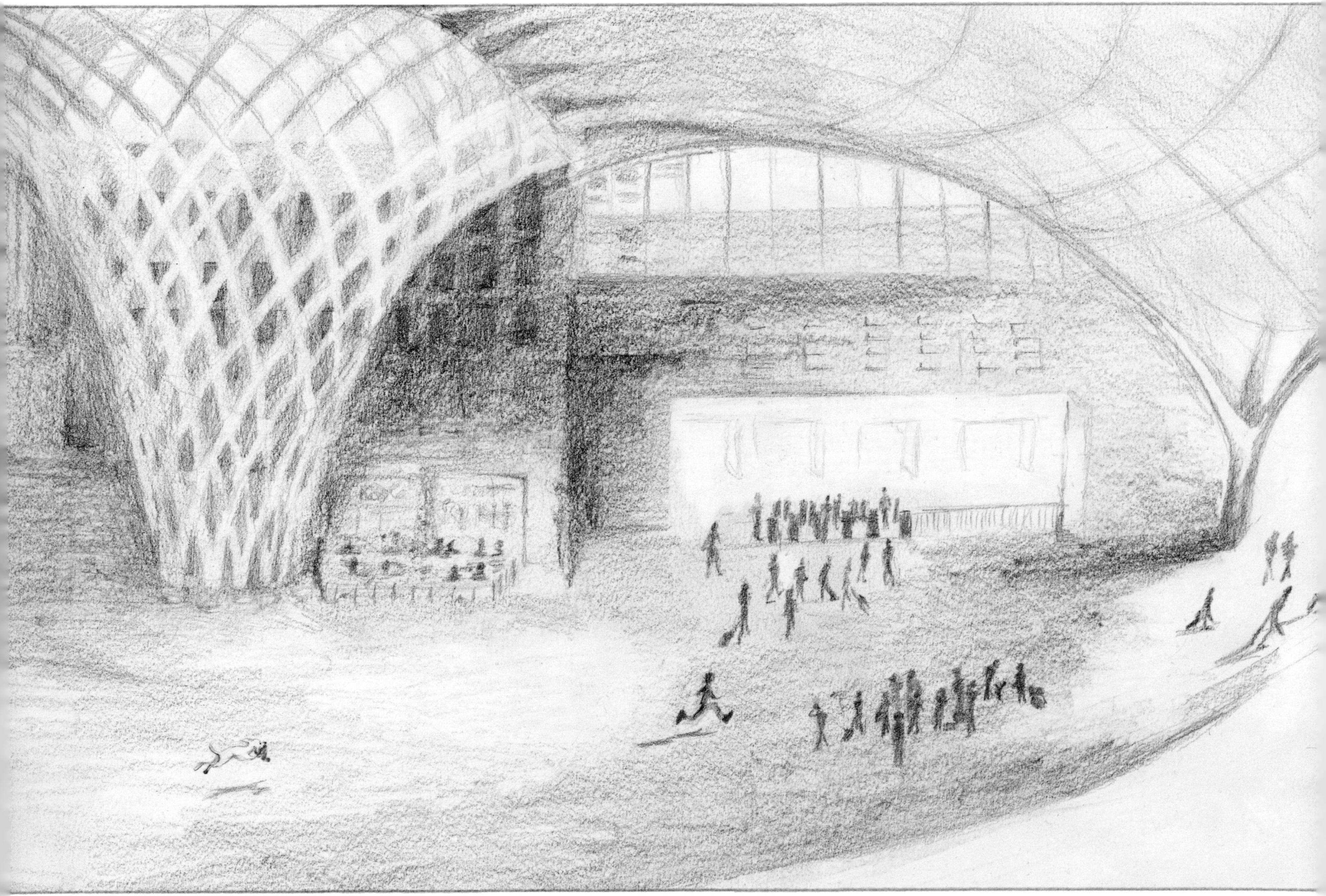

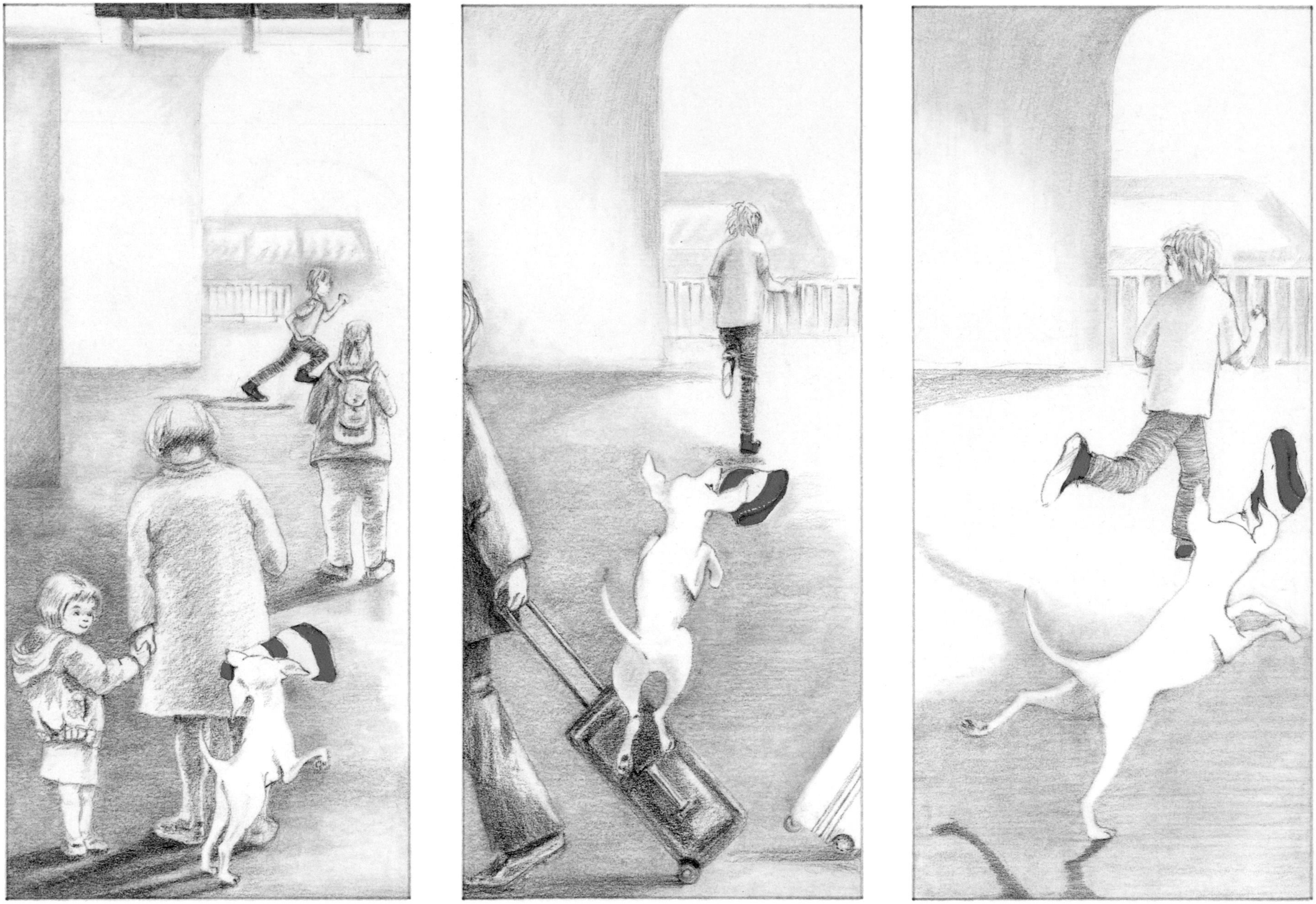

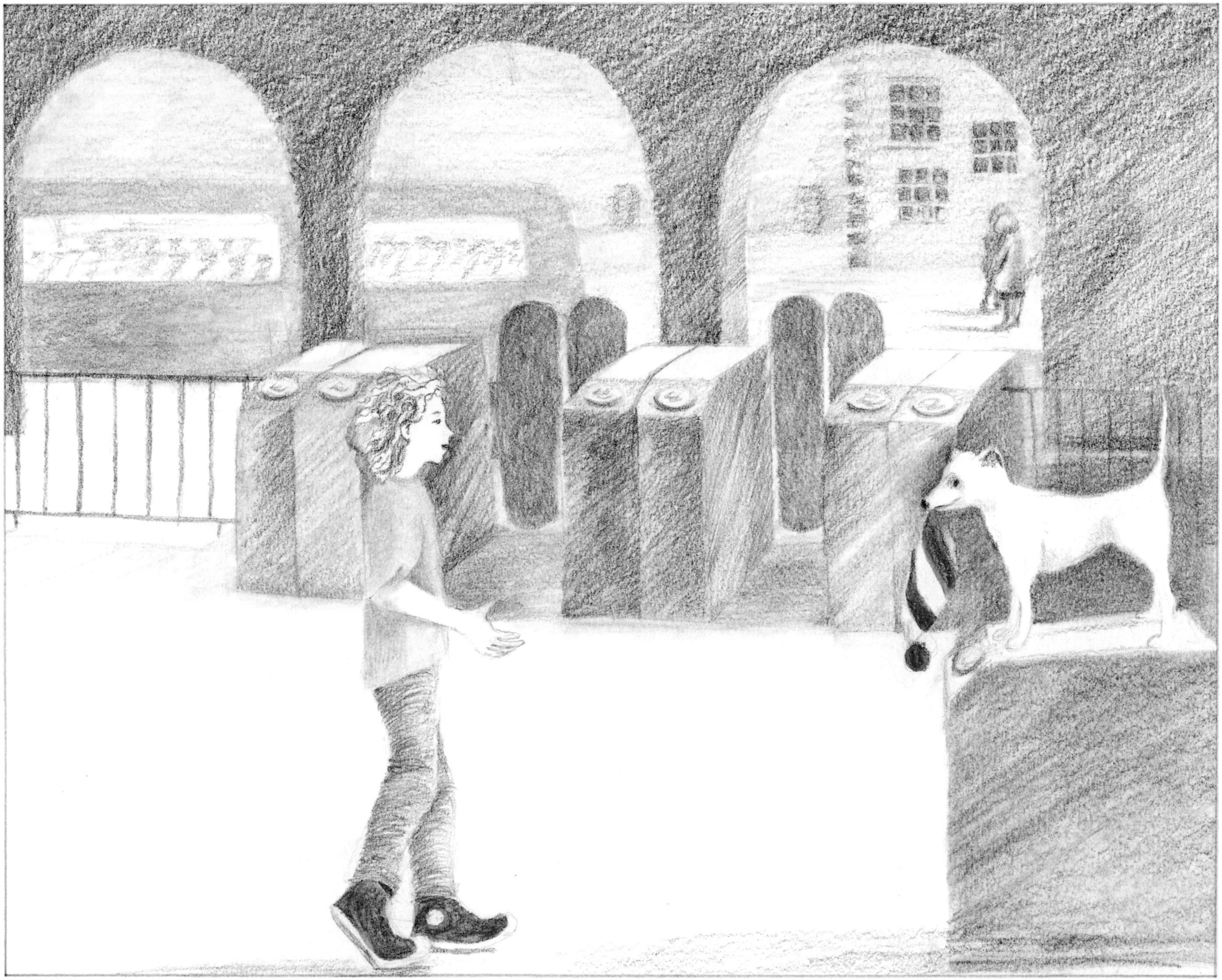

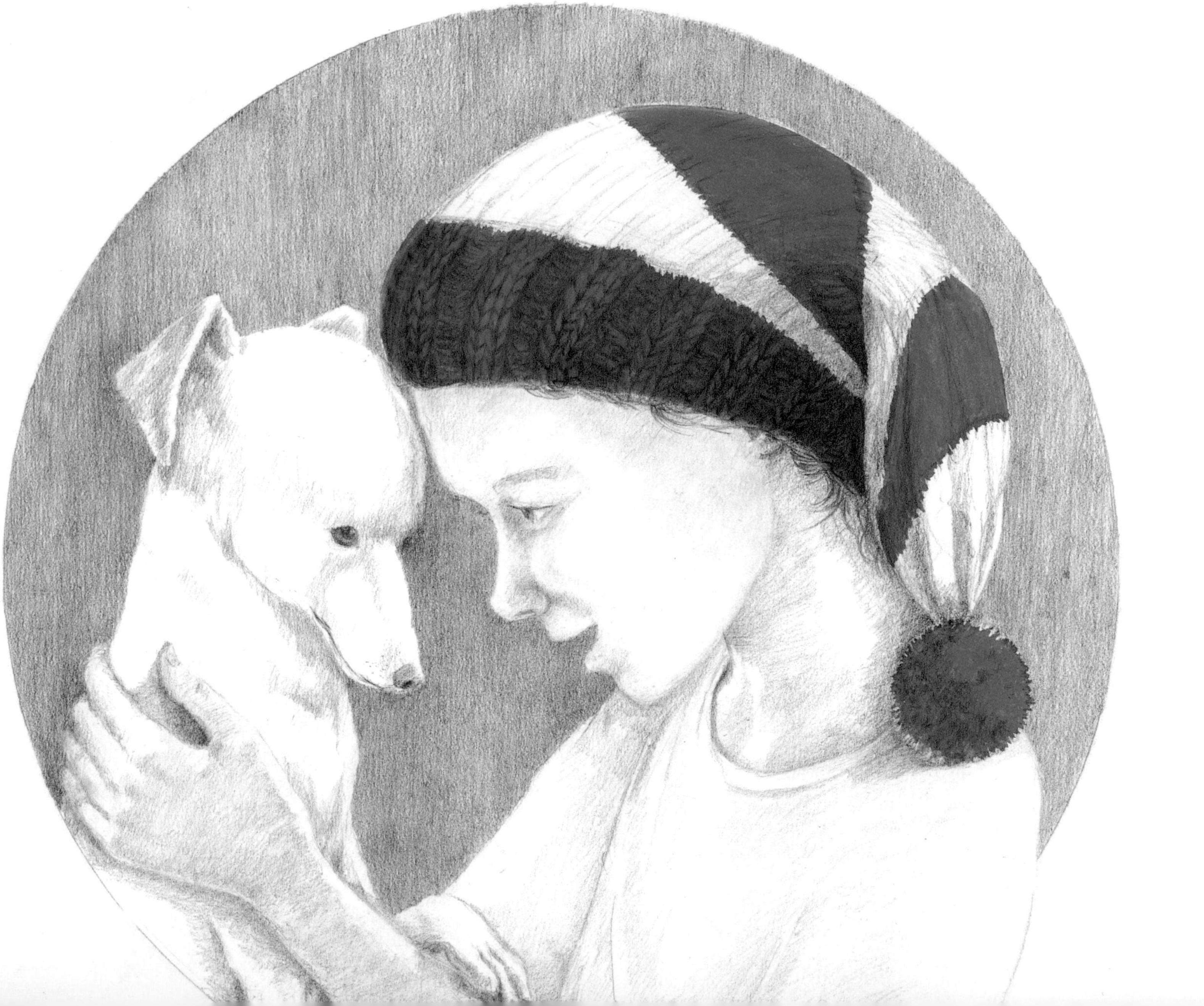